Of
Mrs. Olivia Foxworthy

Written By Alex McLellan

2nd Edition 2020 By Author
ISBN : 9781777112769
Copyright 2020©
Alex McLellan

The Memoirs of Mrs. Olivia Foxworthy Is
A Forest Original Product
&
A Small Potato Production

First Edition Printed
By Sun Rising Poetry Press 2004
ISBN: 0-9755955-4-7
St. Joseph, Missouri, USA

*I dedicate this book to our children,
Amelia & Nathan
with love.*

Contents:

Chapter One p.5
Jedidiah Brown

Chapter Two............................p.25
Sweetest of Angels

Chapter Three..........................p.37
Momma's Tuesday

Chapter Four............................p.68
Cookies From God

Chapter Five............................p.84
All The Difference

Chapter Six..............................p.100
When Clara Laughs

Chapter Seven..........................p.104
Still Something Wanting

Author Notes............................p.115

About The Author....................p.119

Chapter One
Jedidiah Brown

Chapter One
Jedidiah Brown

This is just a short little something about someone who made a difference in my life. Every summer when I was a slip of a child, I stayed with my Aunt Ruth. Now, my Aunt Ruth lived in a small country town that my Father said was backward even though it appeared frontward to me. Coming from the city, it was nice to be in the peaceful country with rolling hills and apple trees. I think most of all I liked the quiet. No motor cars, no hustle and bustle and lots and lots of quiet. I liked the quiet and Jedidiah Brown.

Jedidiah and me were very best friends as friends could be back then. My Aunt Ruth was a lovely lady and I guess if it weren't for her blessing, I'd never have known my Jedidiah. My Uncle was a very nice man, big, strong farmer type. He'd get into my Aunt Ruth about Jedidiah and me. He said my mother would have a full blown fit if she knew what I was getting up to while visiting them. He said, though my Aunt's intentions were good, she couldn't change the world and she should just face facts. My Aunt said it was her God given right to allow me to play with only the best children and Jedidiah was one such child. She said best friends don't grow on trees, and if I was lucky enough to have one great friendship in my life then her fool sister could get stuffed! Her sister...that'd be my mother. All I knew was Jed was there every summer and so was I.

My Momma never met Jedidiah though I spoke of him often. In truth I compared just about every boy I ever met to Jedidiah.

Jedidiah and me met when we were four years old. Jedidiah had a stutter but when he said his name, he never stuttered. His name fit perfectly with his stutter.

By the time we were eight, we were thick as thieves, and Jedidiah had no more stutter.

I loved Jed and he loved me. I told him what my Aunt and Uncle had said and he said his grandparents said the very same thing. He lived with his grandparents and his Momma and Pappa lived in the city.

We had a special spot that was just ours. There was a huge tree that reached over a small hill and we made a lookout where we claimed the land for our own. We tied Jed's hanky to a tall stick and we had a special ceremony and everything.

"We hereby claim this land as Jedidiah and Olivia Country," Jed proudly shouted the announcement while he plunged the stick with 'our flag' into the ground. We stood there for a bit, hands on our hips, admiring our handy work, then we became blood brother and sister and the ceremony seemed perfect. That day was a greater day than we even knew back then.

See, up to now, there was lots of things we hadn't noticed yet. One such thing that might'a been important if we gave a flying stuff, was that my best friend was a boy and his best friend was a girl. That didn't stop us from becoming blood sister and brother. That didn't stop us from lying in the sweet grass side by each and telling each other all our dreams and secrets.

"Olivia, when I grow up, I'm gonna be a doctor."

"When I grow up, I'm gonna be a doctor's wife," I announced confidently. This made Jedidiah smile at me.

I had fallen in love by age ten and there was no use denying it.

Jedidiah was beautiful to me. That fact was the God honest truth of it. Jedidiah had a smile that made me wonder where he put all those perfect teeth when his mouth was closed. He was a strong, fit boy, you know, very athletic, capable. He had a back on him like I'd never seen before. Even his younger brother didn't have a back like Jedidiah, like God carved him out of rock just for me to admire. Jedidiah had a smartness about him, always figuring out stuff. I just loved the looks of him and had made my mind up that he was the finest thing I had ever seen and when I was old enough, I made my mind up to marry that boy. We would rest in the tall sweet grass, laying side by each and talk for hours.

"Jedidiah, when you're a doctor, will you marry me?"

"What are you talking about?"
We both sat up.

"I know you heard me! It's alright with me if I asked you first, cause I reckon I'm a girl who likes to make plans and if you won't have me, I've gotta know."

"Now, Olivia.. I'll always love you, but you and I could never be married. Your Momma would have a fit and my

family would never speak to me again."

Tears welled up and began to pour out.

"Olivia, can we promise to always love each other even when we're old?" Jedidiah asked me with sadness in his voice.

"I don't think I have to promise something like that."

"What do you mean?"

"My heart wouldn't have it any other way," I stated matter of fact like and crossed my arms.

Jedidiah leaned over to me and kissed my cheek. When Jed did that, it always made me smile.

"Maybe by then the world will be different."

Jedidiah lay back with his hands crossed behind his head.

"Just as long as I'm the same," I laid back too looking into the sky for comfort.
"Yeah, me too."
I stretched out with my head on Jed's tummy and we stared up for a long while before heading home that day. Those moments together became so precious to us, more than we could ever know at the time.

That year was the first and only year my mother came to stay with Aunt Ruth for a week before summer ended. I can still see the look on her face the first time she met Jedidiah.
Could'a used a spatula to lift her jaw from the front porch. When shock had finished with her she started scream'n at me. I didn't know what about exactly but I ran to Jedidiah, grabbed him by the hand and we ran to his

house. Coincidentally, his parents were there visiting, preparing to take Jed to live with them.

"Momma, this is Olivia," Jed cordially introduced me.

I smiled politely.

"Pleased to meet you m'am."

Jed's Momma looked confused and his pap looked extremely angry.

"No you don't!" She shouted at Jedidiah.

"Don't what, Momma?"

"Don't you be telling me this, this...girl is the famous Olivia Baker!"

"Is this how you raise a boy? Fill his head with foolish ideas? I just can't believe you two!"

Jed's Pa shouted at his grandparents. Jed's Gramma started to cry when she looked at me and then I looked at Jed and he looked at me, and then we started running.

We were flat out of breath when we arrived at our spot, at our tree.
"Are we in trou-ble!"
"Oh, it's worse than that, Livvy."
"What have we done that's so bad?! Best friends don't grow on trees you know! It's not fair."
"No, it's not fair. But, that's how it is."
"We're never gonna see each other again after this day are we Jedidiah?"
He pulled me close and I breathed him in for the last time.
Our eyes glassed over with tears starting.
"No. But wherever you go, whoever you meet, you'll always have me in your heart."

"Please don't forget me, Jedidiah." I was heartbroken.
"My heart would never let that happen."
"Pinkie swear on our Flags honor?"
"Pinkie swear on our flags honor!"
We held hands until the fork in the road and we went our separate ways, slowly turning back to look until there was nothing more to see.
It was the saddest day of my life. It was as if someone died. Aunt Ruth almost did when my Momma got to shouting at her.
Still, I always wrote letters to Aunt Ruth inquiring about my blood brother, and she'd fill me in every now and then. I heard Jed found himself a wife and had a couple of kids and moved to the city. He was a teacher. I was proud of him. I just

knew he'd be someone worth looking up to.

I married too and had kids. My eldest son's middle name was Marcus, after Jedidiah Marcus Brown.

Many years passed when we got word Aunt Ruth had died and even my mother attended the funeral. There would come a day when I could show my own children my favorite spot where Jed and I played as happy children in a country we created where everyone could be happy. This day was not the appropriate time, but I took a walk by myself and noticed, carved out in the wood of our tree was a heart with mine and Jedidiah's name in it. He'd done that after I left.

Years would pass until I had grandchildren of my own and now I have time to write my memoirs. I

always get lost in those happy days with Jedidiah and me.
One day, I guess a few weeks ago now, a young woman came to my door.
"Excuse me, m'am are you Olivia Baker?"
"Yes, but that was a long time ago."
"May I speak with you?"
"In regards to what young lady?"
"My name is Olivia Brown. Jedidiah Brown was my grandfather."
"Was?"
"Yes,.. He passed on a few weeks back."
"I can't tell you how sorry I am to hear that."
I was shaken. We all know death will find us one day or another, but when it creeps up and catches you off guard, well, it's off putting, startling if you will.

*I invited the lovely young lady in and when she smiled I nearly fell over. "You have your granddad's smile. Sure brings me back a ways."
"Thank you. It would appear that I was named after you and if you don't mind, my grandfather had few things he wanted me to tell you. He left a rather peculiar will. It was wrapped in this dirty, old hanky. He used to carry this hanky around with him everywhere. He never used it, wouldn't wash it, and gave my grandmother a lot of grief over it. He said it would break his heart to part with the old thing. When he died and his will was read, he asked that this old hanky be delivered to you, by me. That was the first I knew of you."
"I'm grateful. It was very kind of you. Your grandfather was the very first love of my life and my first and very*

best friend in the world. If the world was a different place, all our lives would have been different."
"But you're, you're..." the young woman struggled for words in shock.
"Yes, I'm white and Jedidiah was black and no one was happy about two young kids finding each other."
I showed Olivia my memoirs and then she understood. She seemed to have a new love and respect for Jedidiah. When she was about to leave she gave me a letter written by Jed addressed to me.
"I've been instructed to give you this and hold out my hand and ask you to honor this letter in the name of your flag in memory of your country. Do you know what to do, because as God is my witness, I do not?"

"Of course I do, young lady. Pinkie swear." I grabbed her finger and wrapped it around mine.
"You two must'a been crazy!"
After a warm embrace, I asked Olivia for one more of those beautiful smiles. Olivia Brown walked away chuckling to herself.
I didn't read the letter for two full days. Finally, I made myself a cup of tea and sat myself down and began to read.
'Dearest Olivia,
When this letter reaches you I will have passed. I couldn't do that without asking you to marry me the next lifetime we meet. If there is such thing as a next time I'll be looking for you. I hope you have had a wonderful life and it's fair to say I got a few dreams accomplished and have a terrific family. My Olivia will bring

this letter to you and I hope you can take time to tell her about us. I've never forgotten the flag and hope it reaches you. I've never forgotten anything.

I know we were just kids but we had the kind of Big Love that just keeps on going. Now it's your turn not to forget me. When my dear wife died a few years back, I thought of looking you up, but I don't think the world has changed that much yet.

I'll wait for you at "Our Country" by the tree at our special spot. Those slow, breezy days were the happiest of my entire life, Livvy. Over the years, my heart clung to those times and my memories of you to get me through the rough spots. I'll never forget our chance encounter in front of the shop. Hope you still remember. You raised my heart that day, even for as brief a

time as it was. You, your sweet face, you gave me hope in ways you'll never know. I never knew for certain, but I always believed that I might have done the same for you, giving you hope and strength during your life, just knowing The Big Love was real.
I love you, always, dearest Olivia Baker.
I'll be waiting...
Your Jedidiah Brown.'

Oh if only it were true. But it was neither here nor there. It's something I'll look forward to. Oh that day at the shop..my word, what a day that was. I might write that memory up one day.

How I love you still.....Jedidiah Brown.
Always, Olivia.

Entry: 35 this January 5, 1942 Mrs. Olivia Foxworthy.

Chapter Two
Sweetest of Angels

Chapter Two
Sweetest of Angels

There are often times in a woman's life when she may feel deeply and profoundly saddened. Along with all the good there will always be vexation, grief and hard times. Now that my children have asked me to write my memoirs, I realize what a rich life I have lived. I think those kids of mine just wanted to keep me busy, but there's a time for truth in everyone's life and I guess it's just my turn. They'd have to know some time and I suppose now's just as good a time as any. Puts me in mind of that old expression, 'Be careful what you wish for 'cause you just might get it.' This is about grief so bad it could kill someone. It's unimaginable to attempt trying so the way I got through it is to carry it with me and cherish the very thought. It's high time I let my secret out about little Hattie.

Right about now, when you all read this, I can just imagine you all wondering who in the heck little Hattie is, and for good reason. You never knew this little angel, your eldest sister, Harriet Foxworthy. Just when your father and I married, he was notified he'd have to go to war. I just found out I was pregnant and times were hard but we were in love and just starting out, and everything seemed possible when a person is young and in love.

We figured on staying in the city till he left for war and then I'd move in with his parents for the first year till we got properly on our feet. At first, I missed your father terribly. Your grandparents did their best to comfort

me but I soon found I could concentrate on this little bundle of joy growing inside of me and everything seemed almost as it should be.
That's what girls my age did then, got married, started families, and that's how life was. There were thousands of girls in my same predicament. Most of the young men of the country were gone and it seemed everyone left was a mother, sister, grandmother, or mother to be, and we were without our fathers, sons, and husbands.

Finally the day came and Hattie Foxworthy was born. Oh she was just beautiful. The first time your father set eyes on her I swear he fell in love. That means an awful lot to a young woman to see the man she loves so devoted to the child she herself would die for.

It was wonderful, but short-lived, our time we three spent together that is. It seemed only moments had passed and your father was off to an uncertain future and I was left for a longer stay than intended with your grandparents. When grandpa took ill, our future seemed even more less than certain. Grandma took on the care of Hattie and I went to one of factories and became a worker. Women were dropping like flies from exhaustion. They could really work us and my heavens, was it hot! Took everything I had to keep that job. I started at five in the morning and I worked all the whole day and didn't see my Hattie until night came. I was so sad to leave her every day. Oh things were so different then. Today, people, workers get coffee breaks, telephone privileges, raises, benefits and such privileges, but back then, you just had to keep sewing those damn uniforms for our men and boys to go get killed in. Every soldier that was found dead needed a uniform to be buried in. Seemed the dead ones needed uniforms as much as the live ones. It was just terrible. You ate in the morning and then again at night. That's how life was and grandma took ill soon herself caring for grandpa and Hattie. There was just so little money, and no work. I had one of the few jobs. That time in my life seemed so hopeless to me. I didn't know what to do more than I was already doing. So I went to work and all day I drummed up enough courage to hope life would be better tomorrow and my little Hattie, well she grew without me. At least she was well loved and taken care of.

I was depressed in a way that exhaustion can cause and everyone being in the same boat, I was sad, feeling unable to cope, and I missed my husband, and my baby.
One evening following work, I dragged myself wearily home. Everyone walked back then, however far it was, not like today. Sometimes I think that slow walk home saved my life, letting me feel the sun setting on my face reminded me I was alive. When I turned the corner and headed down the street toward the house, first thing I noticed was that horrible smell. Then I saw thick smoke that billowed way up into the heavens. My heart pounded. It wasn't until I got closer down that street I realized the smoke carried my little girl with it. It was just the sort of thing you knew without being told.

A crowd of neighbors gathered round the house and they parted as they saw me walk toward it. I swear I was on my way into that house to get my child even though I knew it was too late. I dropped my bags and was making my way in when a fireman stopped me. He ushered me over to the sidewalk and sat me down. He waved to another fireman who brought a blanket with him. It was brown with smoke. I held the blanket up to my face. It was still warm from the fire and through it all, I could smell her smell, that clean, just been washed lavender smell. I clutched that blanket like a crazy woman. It was all I had. I ran my finger over the corner of her blanket that had a tiny square piece cut out that I stitched over so it wouldn't fray as I had used that piece to mend Hattie's little sweater. Oh, my Lord! My Little Angel was really gone...

The fireman met my eyes and swallowed hard as he took my hand and whispered, "There ain't nothing left of anything, Ma'm. I'm so sorry for your loss."

I broke his stare and looked to the sky as my eyes burned with my sorrow. My loss! What in heaven's name did this man know about my loss?! Nothing!

I thought that at least if things really do happen for a reason, Hattie would have her grandparents to take good care of her up in heaven. That's how I got through it. That's how I stood at those three graves and prayed for them to always be together. That's how I was able to write your father...it's called hope in the faith that there's more to know, more to love, that there's just plain old more…

In those days, a city block was all row housing and if one caught fire, they were all pretty much gone. Many people died that day including children. It was a terrible tragedy. Your father felt utterly and completely helpless being so far away and unable to comfort me. In some ways it seemed to him that war is just so wrong, accidents like this was just God's way of evening out the playing field. He was very bitter until you children came along and life seemed to get better slowly. They say time heals all wounds but I don't think this kind of thing falls under that category. Since these are my memoirs, that's how I see it and you all should know that there were always four of you in my heart your whole lives. I think of little Hattie often and when my own first grandchild came along, you can bet how serious I took on that responsibility.

I suppose I must be wise and flower you with my accumulated knowledge that someone my age ought to know, but I can't. I have no idea why things happen. I have no idea how we all survived the war, the hunger, the incredible loss...I just don't know how we did it, but we did and you three are here today because we kept on. The next time one of your kids demands new shoes, you tell'm to earn them because they can, and they deserve to know what will and trying can get done.

We didn't have the luxury of going to anyone to demand anything. To be honest, I wouldn't wish my hardship

on anyone. But, if anyone reads these words I've written, if anyone takes the time to know what it was like for me, they just ought to know, I squeezed every drop of joy into my life I could, I laughed whenever I got the chance, and did my best to look people in the eyes, had a firm hand shake, and to my knowledge never went out of my way to do anything to someone I wouldn't like done to myself.
Well, except that one time but I haven't decided whether I should write about that yet.

Entry: 37 this January 28, 1942 Mrs. Olivia Foxworthy

Chapter Three
Momma's Tuesday

Chapter Three
Momma's Tuesday

Back when you children were just very small, your grandmother, my mother, came to live with us, much against your father's will. He figured there should be a place for crazy old people so as not to burden them on their children. There were hospitals for the sick, but the old and not quite right in head ones went to their children. I remember my Aunt Ruth once told me that you don't get to pick your relations and good or bad, you always own them. Live with us she did and she brought that damn dog, Foalie Two with her.
What a handful! I swear it was like having one more child around. I can't say what was more annoying to me, the money game or that damn dog

squat'n and doing his business right in the house.

Your Gramma would sit on the porch swing or on the bench in the back yard and play the money game with you. In the beginning, it was curious to me in an endearing sort of humorous way, but when I realized she was serious, the whole thing was quite a horse of a different color.

One morning I was hanging the laundry on the line and I could see Gramma sit'n on a table cloth on the lawn hav'n herself a little picnic with you children. She was playing the money game.

"Now children, what are you going to do with your share of the money?"

That damn mongrel dog Foalie Two was sitting right with her. He'd never leave her side.

One of you was going to buy a big new house, one of you was going to sail the world, one of you wanted all the chocolate candy you could buy, and then came the big question, "Now which one of you will care for Foalie Two?"
All of you wanted that damn dog and then she'd tell you, "Your Momma, would never allow it! Even if I gave you all my share of the money!
Oh well, guess not much can be done, Foalie Two."
I dropped what I was doing and marched right over there to make my feelings known.
"Now Momma! Playing games is one thing, but stop filling the children's heads with wild notions about money! We are not wealthy, never have been and never will be! And as for that damn mongrel with the damn foolish

name, well he does his business wherever he feels like! Who names their dog Foalie Two? What kind of fool name is that?!"

"Now Olivia, Foalie Two is downright insulted! He's got a fine name. And as for this mood you find yourself in, your march your rude self right into the house and don't speak to any of us at this fine picnic until you can compose yourself!"
You children giggled seeing someone treat your mother like a child and in that heat I raised my arms in the air, "Momma, what am I going to do with yah?"
I turned and started to walk off and I could hear her whispering, which I also think is a nasty habit in the presence of others.

"Now, did you know if you wean puppies too soon from their mothers they can get very cross later on and some get so bad they have to be put down?"

"No, Gramma, we didn't know that."

"Well, some say, I weaned your Momma a might too soon and so we'll have to wait and see what happens."

All you children looked over to me and then you burst out laughing. I was so frustrated, I stomped over to that laundry basket and gave it a big kick as I followed my mother's instructions and marched into the house.

As the days wore on, your Grandmother regressed at a steady pace and Doc Williams said he gave her a couple of months at best. She began to not know where she was, some days didn't know who she was

but she never forgot that damn dog! He has been a thorn in my side for most of my life. I just never took to my mother's dog. He was fairly good natured but crotchety like my mother. One night I remember bringing my mother a cup of tea after dinner. She was bed ridden at this point and didn't know one day from the next.
"Momma, brought you some tea."
"Oh good, Tuesday. That other girl can't get her head out of her butt long enough to even bring me some dinner."
"Excuse me?!"
"Just put it over here, Tuesday. Come on up here beside me Foalie."
"Momma, as long as I've ever known him, you've called him Foalie Two?"
"Tuesday? Have you had too much sun today?"

I sent for Doc Williams and he explained that at this point in her mind's memory, she'll often recount days from her own past. He said that I should just try to get along with her and if she thinks I'm someone named Tuesday, then I'd best be Tuesday. So there I was for three weeks answering to the name of Tuesday, minding that fool dog Foalie Two.

After a particularly long night tending to my mother's needs, my neighbor, Charlene took you young ones for the morning. I went into my mother's room and she lay in bed humming a song I never heard before that day, just staring out the window. I looked at her real close like and for just a moment I could see her as a little girl. She turned and smiled. I smiled back.
"Tuesday?"
"Yes."

"Don't you miss your home, Tuesday?"
"Yes."
"What are you going to do with your share of the money? I'm going to buy myself a dog. Haven't picked a name yet but you can be sure it'll be something special."
"I'm going to keep it all for myself."
"Oh, Tuesday, you are so funny. Your Pap will need some of your share for sure, now won't he! My Pah already has things set up for him. Things are in his name. Now why are you surprised, Tuesday? That's how things should be. When your Pap is a free man, then he can buy your Momma outright! Won't that be fine! Then we can always play together whenever we want. Now, don't cry Tuesday. I won't be sickly forever.

This fever will pass and then you and me can go swimming again."

I felt as though I were right inside her head. Maybe all of this was real. Maybe Momma did have a friend named Tuesday when she was a child.
"Oh, I don't know about things the way you do," I kept the conversation going.
"Yes sir! No flies on you! I taught you to read and you all but out done me on my spelling! Now Tuesday, let's make plans like we always do about the money. We'll buy matching dresses. Oh, and our hats will have to be matching and real big like so everyone will see how rich we are from the Tobacco. Tuesday, I do declare you quite rude falling asleep like that!"
"Oh excuse me."

"It's alright for now but you just march right out there and tell Foalie not to work you so hard because you are too tired to talk to me!"

"Foalie is a man?" I was astonished.

"Well, he's your father! You ought'a know it! What in heaven's name got into you Tuesday?"

"Guess I must be tired."

"Foalie! Foalie! You get yourself in here right now!"

"He's gone for the day." I said calmly.

"When he gets back, I'll give him a piece of my mind, but for now I'm tired. Thank you Tuesday for spending time with me."

"Oh it's quite alright. How's my Pap ever gonna get that kind a money? People round here won't like that sort of thing happening," I asked out of curiosity.

"My Pah has a plan. Your Pap may seem like a slave, but he isn't. Get it like? It's a secret. Everything will carry on just like always. No one will be the wiser. When your Momma comes, it'll be like my Pah bought her but really, your Pap did and the same for you and your brothers too. You own your own land, your own house, just like how it ought'a be. Oh isn't it wonderful? They thought I was asleep. I heard the whole thing. Oh Tuesday, good night now..."
"Goodnight..."
My Momma drifted off asleep with her secrets and that damn dog Foalie Two right beside her. In a few short hours she was gone forever and that damn dog too. So devoted, he died. Of course he did his business right there on the bed beside her in his basket

before he died, but he died, so I guess beggars can't be choosers.

It was a sad time for a day, as people faded in and out of the funeral parlor. Some strangers, some old faces I hadn't seen for some time passed. Things really got confusing at the reading of the will. There I sat with my husband and you children in front of the lawyer and nothing on heaven and earth could have ever prepared me for the notion...Things to be done? The Lawyer read aloud.

"Being of sound mind and body, I leave my entire estate to my daughter, Mrs. Olivia Foxworthy. She will be responsible for carrying out my will explicitly and without exclusion of any detail."

And there were many, many details! So there I was about to go on a pilgrimage, as per instructions to visit

my Uncle, my Aunt Ruth's husband, to a place I hadn't been since my Aunt died. I arrived to find my Uncle in very high spirits as usual.
"So Olivia, she finally kicked it?"
"Good to see you too."
We chatted and then finally he said it was time I knew the truth. To get that I had to meet someone I never knew the whole of my life.
Mrs. Ginger Pennyroyal was a very striking black lady who ran the general store. She seemed a little older than myself. My Uncle who was in a wheel chair by now, gave her a big hug when they saw each other.
"Ginger, this is Olivia."
"Pleased to meet you. You bear a striking resemblance to your grandmother and your Aunt Ruth."
"Thank you, I'm sure."

"Oh yes, the whole Jed thing way back then, I remember now."
My Uncle shook his head sadly remembering.
"Well enough of that. Your Uncle tells me you are the one to put things right finally."
"I am just following the peculiar directions of my mother's will."
"Well, have a seat young lady. Have we got something in store for you."
"I knew this day would come. Wish my Ruthy was here to see it!" My Uncle wiped a tear from his eye with his hanky.
"Now you don't doubt for one moment that she isn't," Ginger reassured patting his hands compassionately.
I was beginning to get a tad nervous with these two. Mrs. Pennyroyal sat

down slowly. She seemed to choose her words very carefully.

"Olivia, you come from a long line of carefully guarded secrets and very good people, your grandfather, Jonas, amongst them, was one of the best of men. He had insight into humanity in a way that was far ahead of his time and he died working hard for what he believed in."

"He believed in corn?" I couldn't imagine what this had to do with Jonas, a corn farmer.

"This is going to be harder than I thought," Ginger sighed.

"Don't I know it!" my Uncle added, "Couldn't believe it myself when I heard it."

"Back when your grandfather was establishing himself here, it was customary to buy black slaves to work your land for you, keep house, do the

dirty work. Jonas was no different and bought quite a few over the years and was well respected for it by other whites. He was also well respected by blacks and everyone wanted to work for him. He was fair, decent, honest and it was a safe place, not like others. Some women were raped, beaten, killed back then, and nothing but hard work ever went on at your Grandfather's. I know you don't hear much about him, because he died when your mother and your Aunt were not quite full-grown. It was tobacco he grew, not corn. He owned over fifty slaves and freed more than double that amount before he died and even more after he died. He was a good man, Olivia.

Your grandmother on the other hand, well, she was a piece of work. Edith, was cross it seemed, but good at heart and in the end, things came right by her as well. Jonas had developed a scheme where his slaves worked on his land and earned their freedom, bought their own homes, raised their own families, and all was in secret. His land was very prosperous and the money rolled in, not just for him, but for all his workers. See, back then there was no such thing as "free" slaves. A white man could be killed and his family destroyed for even having the thought. Everyone knew the stakes were high, but Jonas insisted this was the way to go. He didn't see things the way everyone else did and this is what killed him, all his hard work. As years passed, he began to set up bank accounts in his house and people began saving money, just like at the bank. Life seemed great back then. Everything

was legal and everything was in writing.
As years passed, freeing slaves became more and more heard of and less and less popular. One of Jonas' long- time friends and employees, was Foalie. They had known each other forever and Foalie was owned by Jonas. He was one of the first ever bought and freed. Foalie would have died for Jonas and likewise. Foalie used to joke that he would die for him any day of the week except Tuesday. Tuesday was payday and he'd be more than willing to die the day after. Foalie had a daughter with him at one point. A pretty little thing and she was born on a Tuesday. It was payday and seemed just as good a name as any. Tuesday and your own Momma were childhood best friends. Tuesday's Momma worked at the plantation in

the next county and though they refused to sell her, Jonas was able to buy Foalie's children. Of course, it was really Foalie who bought their freedom all along. No one knew that. Even Foalie appeared to be owned for most of his life. This way, he couldn't be sold even if something happened to Jonas."

"Foalie was a man!" I whispered.

"Yeah, that poor Momma of yours. How she suffered. I heard she called her dog Foalie out of love and respect and when that one died, she called the next one Foalie Two."

"You have always known? No one ever breathed a word." I couldn't believe it.

"Please try and understand. I know it's difficult to take in all at once. Lives were at stake and times were very volatile.

Your Momma wasn't racist. I know you and she had difference of opinion, especially over Jed. Life doesn't exclude anyone from pain, Olivia. She was bitter. See, she was stricken with the brain fever when she was a child and if it wasn't for her and the way things happened, you and I might not be sitting here today. Maybe we should walk a ways."

We walked to the graveyard. The sun was bright and the day was hot and dry. Ginger kept a steady pace and walked with an air that seemed almost regal. I can remember thinking how well her name suited her. Ginger Pennyroyal was perhaps the most graceful woman I had ever met. We sat on a wooden bench and she continued.

"If Jonas had ever been found out, it would have all been over. Foalie

would have been killed and so would everyone who had ever known anything about it. One night, Mr. Haggerty, a local seed man, got into the alcohol and decided to pay Jonas a visit and see where all the money was. Jonas didn't believe in banks and everyone knew it. He lived modestly but he was clearly successful and Mr. Haggerty burst into the house with a couple of others, shot guns in hand and they were riled, ready to shoot someone.

People had been noticing Foalie looking quite well lately and he had a way about him, like he was proud. White men hated that. Jonas told him but he wouldn't listen. Jonas told him to know what good he was doing would have to be enough, not to go around giving people the wrong idea. Haggerty started thinking that Jonas was up to something. He dragged Jonas and Foalie out of their houses. All the noise disturbed your Momma. Full of fever, she rose out of bed, walked slowly out into the yard and shouted, "I can't get any sleep! Foalie! Foalie, do you hear me?! You can work day and night if you want to, but if you have time to play dress up wearing my Pah's new shirt and walk around town like you own the place, then surely Tuesday can spend some time taking care of me! She plum fell asleep bringing me my tea! Take that fool shirt off and put your regular clothes on. You'll get to giving everyone the wrong idea about us all out here." She was in her night gown and she took Foalie by the hand and led him into the house shouting at him the whole way. "Foalie, if you behave yourself, I'll name my dog after you.

Would you like that Foalie?" Even Haggerty burst out laughing at the idea Jonas was 'letting' Foalie have money. Foalie lowered his head and followed your mother into the house like a slave would.
She saved lives that night and she didn't even know it. She didn't even remember the night at all. By the time she came out of her fever, many things had changed. Tuesday was nowhere to be found. Your Momma was given a mongrel puppy she named Foalie, to help her recover from fever and the loss of Tuesday, which was never explained. She always thought Tuesday ran off to be with her mother. Tuesday was your Momma's best friend in the world and after losing her, she became bitter and crotchety like Edith. See, she had taught Tuesday to read and write and

secretly expected a letter or something, poor little heart to keep hoping like that. When your grandfather died, he had enough money to get by but instead of being a millionaire, which he could have been, he settled for well off and he had Foalie continue the secret. It just takes one man with an idea and sometimes one very spoiled, outspoken little girl with a best friend and few dreams to make all the difference in the world."

"Aside from being admittedly surprised my Momma was no racist, that Jonas freed slaves by the hundreds, and now knowing she named her dogs out of her love for Foalie who was real, I still do not understand the peculiar instructions of her will."

"Well, secrets have a way of finding the light even if it takes generations to get there. One more thing, and then the will.

See, it wasn't until your Aunt Ruth died that your Momma noticed something she'd walked by millions of times and never noticed before. I think some things changed for her after that visit. Come on now, and stand right here."

I stood on a small part of grass and looked down to see a very tiny, flat cemetery stone with two faintly carved words, "Tuesday's Free".

I looked to Ginger.

"Tuesday didn't leave. She died. She refused to leave your Mother's side. She wore herself thin. When she caught brain fever, it took her fast. No one had the heart to tell your mother. Perhaps that was a mistake, maybe

not. Tuesday died a free child in her own right in the arms of her father with his dear friend Jonas at his side. She died free and literate. Do you know how rare a thing that was?"
I began to cry. I understood my mother so much better now. I even felt bad for disliking Foalie knowing more about him. Ginger stood beside me and gave me a tissue.
"Dry your eyes. It's all for the best. Along with the bad came the good. When Ruth died, your Momma carried the load of the secrets on her shoulders."
I drew a deep breath and looked into the distance. The town was small and I could see the general store. The awning blew gently in the wind and I could see the wooden sign above the store in bold letters. It read, "Tuesdays".

"Yah see now? Your own Momma did that for her dear friend with some of her share of her money."
I cried never knowing. I looked to Ginger and she put her arm around me. "It'll be o.k. Olivia. Things just take time."
I hugged Ginger then. I looked into her eyes.
"I see, now just who the hell am I to know all of these going's on while you didn't?"
"Yes, I suppose..."
"I'm the one who had to carry the secret in my family. Mrs.Olivia Foxworthy, allow me to introduce myself as the granddaughter of Jonas's best friend in the world, old Foalie."

I smiled as the rest of the instructions seemed to make perfect sense now. It would appear the money game was real. I met with attorneys and we settled land titles, turned over assets, and agreed on fair amounts of inherited wealth. Seems my generation was the safest of decades to do this sort of thing yet. No one involved went away empty handed and in the end there was still quite a lot of money to be had by all. Strange to me was the idea you can know someone your whole life and never know them at all. I did however feel honored to be the one to sign papers and be a part of such a noble cause in any small way.

On the bus ride home, back to reality, which incidentally looked very different now, the voices of two little girls giggling about the wealth they would acquire sang out in my mind.

That was the trip I returned from with special presents, you may recall. A very large box of chocolates, a sailing ship, and a huge doll house all for you kids to help you out with the money game. When your father saw me come through the door I thought he was going to pop a gasket. We never spent money like that. I don't suppose we had seen his eyebrows squeeze together that intensely before. One of you leaned into the other and said, "He was probably weaned too soon like Momma was! We'll have to wait and see what happens!"
That was the second time your father's eyebrows ever squeezed together that way. He never was any good with change or the confusing. You kids high-tailed it out'a there just in case. Things came right shortly after a brief conversation explaining

the almost unbelievable. Even your father's face relaxed after a while. I can't say I recall his eyebrows ever returning to that awkward position again...Oh yes, but I still haven't decided to write about that yet either.

Entry: 38 this February 4,1942
Mrs. Olivia Foxworthy

Chapter Four
Cookies From God

Memoirs of Mrs. Olivia Foxworthy
Cookies From God

There comes a time in everyone's life when one just has to do what's right and that's it! I wasn't sure if I should write all this down for my grandchildren to read some day, but then I decided it would explain a few things about my faith in God.
When you children were growing up, it was customary that the mothers of children attending school would provide baked goods to raise money for school events. I always baked the same thing just to save face and get rid of the task at hand while donating something. I really felt busy enough and was bothered to do extra on occasion.

When you're just minding your own business, and someone has to go out of their way to point you out, it's a very clear indication that God has a definite plan somewhere acting itself out.
I've never been one for crowds. I don't much like making a spectacle of myself.
Now that having been stated, I guess I can present my case.
First I'd like to say, I'm not especially proud of my actions. Though not dishonest, they were not exactly honest. Secondly, I'd like to say that perhaps I should have handled things in a more lady like fashion. Thirdly, I'd like it to be on record that if I could do it all over again, I probably would do the exact same thing!
It was Christmas. The lady's school auxiliary was always planning this

and that ahead of time. I never attended any meetings, never once expressed any interest in the organization and I always donated some baking when asked. Far as I was concerned, the needs of my family came first. Though school morale was always a concern of the auxiliary, I felt I contributed in my own way and that would have to be good enough. I always made up a batch of Oatmeal cookies and those lady's, one in particular, always looked like she had a permanent bad smell under her nose. They always put pressure on me because they felt I should help out more, my having more than one child attending the school. So this year I had my fill!

I attended a Christmas play you children were performing in. We all had to sign in and then deliver our

baking to the table for the gathering that always followed the play.
"Good evening Mrs. Foxworthy."
She greeted me with her usual snootiness.
"Good evening Mrs. Walters."
I maintained cordial behavior.
"I see you have brought your usual meager contribution for the table? Can I put you down for next week's function as well? Only one dozen Oatmeal cookies?"
"Yes, if you would be so kind."
"Thank you so much."
Mr. Walters seemed embarrassed at his wife's brashness.
"Now, Mable,"
"Shush now," *She answered back as he rolled his eyes in an irritated fashion.*
When I tell you that woman got under my skin, I'd be telling it mild like.

Your father said that was just her way and I should rise above it, let it roll off me. There was no reason for it. Why should she care to be publicly so rude to me? I made my mind up to not make the usual oatmeal cookies and thought I'd try chocolate chip. Since I couldn't find fault with myself, I thought she must dislike oatmeal. That was my easy remedy and I swear to God as my witness, that was my plan to make my life a tad more pleasant when I had to expose myself to the likes of Mrs. Mable Walters! Better than that, I was going to have her over for tea figuring I would let her get to know me a little better and that would help matters when in public. You know that expression, 'Timing is everything?' Well, it's especially true in this case.

As planned, Mrs. Walters arrived on that fateful Friday afternoon and we had tea and chocolate chip cookies. I didn't actually eat any because I had been watching my figure, but they were a hit! Mable Walters loved them! We chatted politely and she confessed she wished I would broaden my baking contributions instead of donating the same old thing all the time. Eager to rectify any mistaken hostilities, I readily agreed. All in all I was quite pleased with the afternoon and we parted without incident. I was relieved to tell her I would be happy to see her that very evening for the children's Christmas singing performance and I would bring my chocolate chip cookies.

Upon arriving Mrs. Walters greeted me in a most friendly fashion asking me for the recipe for my cookies. She

*gently but assertively grabbed the plate of cookies as we spoke.
"I'll see these get where they are going, Olivia."*

She was especially interested in the type of chocolate chips as they were very tasty. It was a basic cookie recipe with a little extra brown sugar and I actually just chop up whatever chocolate bar is around the house. She was very surprised. I can't tell you the relief I felt! I became quite pleased with myself. Such a simple solution. I felt like a genius! She liked the cookies so much, she took them home with her and didn't leave them on the table for the children to share. Every Saturday morning, Mrs. Walters has a morning walk with her dog who happens to look just like her, nose in the air, and funny little waddle. This Saturday, she was

nowhere to be seen. Sunday arrives and with Christmas right around the corner, we are all in pretty good spirits.
Things were running smoothly until your father can't find something gravely important. He's in a panic because he can't find his chocolate bar and he was rummaging through the cupboards like a crazy man.
"Where is it?!"
"That chocolate bar?"
"Yes, damn it!"
"No sense cussing around the children!"
"But I specifically told all of them it wasn't to be eaten! It's special!"
"Aren't they all!"
"Please not now woman! You have no idea how I need that chocolate bar!"
"Children, wait out on the walk please."

Soon as you were out the house, your father told me the most bizarre thing.
"Now what are you going on about?"
"Oh Olivia! Not now! Can't you see I'm in agony over here?"
He was holding his stomach with one hand and tapping his behind with the other.
"Oh my God! What can be the matter with you?"
"Remember I said Wilber drummed up a little something for me so I could take my laxatives to work in front of the guys?"
"Yeah..."
"Well, he made them into two chocolate bars for me. Now I can't find it and I got to go and I mean bad like, but I need that damn bar. Now where is it?"
I just bit my lower lip and then he knew I was in a pickle of some kind.

"Livvy, what have you done with my laxative? I'm dying over here!"
"Oh my goodness! Take your regular stuff for now love, and we'll look for it later."
I rushed out of there as fast as I could. I headed over to Wilber's house and luckily he had made up a couple more. Then we headed on over to the church. I couldn't wait to get there to ask forgiveness. I realized poor Mable must have just made it home on time, and come to think, I hadn't seen her on her usual walk first thing the next morning. She also hadn't spent any time lingering after the show. Oh my heavens, what had I done?
Well, when we arrived at church, I began praying immediately. I couldn't pump out those Hail Mary's quick enough! I was positively sweating. I

noticed Mr. Walters entering the church and he walked directly up to my pew and tapped me on the shoulder.

"Mrs. Olivia Foxworthy?"

"Why, Mr. Walters. Good to see you."

"Yes indeed. I would very much like to speak with you in regards to my wife after the service if you don't mind."

"Of course."

"Thank you kindly."

So I planned on doing the right thing. I rehearsed what I'd say. I decided to tell the exact truth and hope there were no hard feelings. Mind you, Mable had eaten the contents of a whole chocolate bar. That was a week's worth. She'd eaten the whole batch I was betting. Oh my word! Though she had been so rude these

past years, even Mable didn't deserve leaky bum. I think I must have been scared at the moment service ended because I found myself wondering just how fast I could run home without being noticed. I walked slowly. With you children already out the church doors I was hoping Mr. Walters would forget.
"Oh, Mrs.Foxworthy!"
I looked back and he waved me over to him. I clutched my pocketbook with the evidence in tow.
"Mr. Walters. Where is your charming wife?"
"That's what I need to speak with you about."
"She's not taken ill, I hope?"
"Oh, on the contrary! She would like me to thank you on her behalf. Something in those cookies... She's always con-...Well let's just suffice to

say she's the happiest she's been in years thanks to you. I'd like to thank you as well because when she's happy so am I, if you get my meaning. Keep those cookies coming!"

I was in shock. Who would have imagined? My word! What a relief! As time passed Mrs. Mable Walters and I became quite familiar acquaintances and I was on my way to my new dilemma.

Every week for two years I made a batch of cookies and it wasn't until the day the Walters were to move to a new city that I confessed my secret. At this point, Mable didn't care because she felt so much better. I can see how one could be irritable living in that condition for years. I can see how easy it was for me to make the mistake of using the chocolate bar for my baking. I can even see how, somehow

God just knew to work through me in that way. One thing I'll never know is just how coincidence works so well. I am a big believer in the idea there is always more to know. I passed it on to my own kids and they passed it on to my grandchildren. That should explain why my children always try to do their best and be their best.
I still feel dishonest for not having told Mable right away. I am not particularly proud of one other fact, which is why I could not decide to write this. I know God works in mysterious ways. I know he has woven many a plan to act itself out in the great fabric of our lives. I do confess, I am to this day, quite pleased his mysterious plan involving Mrs. Mable Walters and a whole load of laxatives!

So in a way they really were Cookies from God!
As my dear friend Ethel would have said, "Guess it all worked out in the end!"

Entry 39 This March 22, 1942
Mrs. Olivia Foxworthy

Chapter Five
All The Difference

Chapter Five
All the Difference

When Abby first asked me to write my memoirs, I knew it was to keep an old fool busy. Somehow children always get to thinking peculiar things about the parent who lives when the other parent dies. Suddenly, I needed to be kept busy. I am however exceedingly grateful none of you children ever thought to buy me a damn mongrel dog like Foalie Two!
I know you children love me and I guess I can tell you I get lonely sometimes, but I'm happy. That can make all the difference to an old person after their spouse of many years passes. I'm plain old happy! See, I've lived well, loved well and I have been truly loved. Every woman should be loved well, know what it is

to love and be loved, truly, not like what young people get up to today. See, when I look back, I look back fondly. My first love I ever had, stayed with me so well, I had a frame of reference as an adult. Your father, believe me, met every standard I set. I think he was the best man I ever knew. He was kind and a great father. He was a strong man with a good heart and a will of iron. 'Course he did on occasion, lose his temper but even then, things never got out of control. He was decent and I loved him so. I love him just the same every day until, under God's guidance, we'll meet again.
Now let's see… Oh yes. Ethel Cosburn. Ethel is my best friend. We've known each other since we were fifteen. When I tell you she was like kin to me, I'd be saying it lightly.

We were thick as thieves. Oh the times we had! She is the type of friend that never leaves even if she lives somewhere different from you. We even married within months of each other. She married a wonderful man named Bun short for Bartholomew. As she and I began our married lives, we drifted apart geographically, but our hearts were so familiar, whenever we saw each other again, it was like we had never been apart. Right after I married your father, I moved to the city and within a very short time, Hattie arrived. Ethel had Bart Jr. and that was the last I heard for some time. We were so poor then, I never even dreamed of sending letters. That privilege was reserved for those who could afford stamps. Well after Hattie and all that, a full five years passed and Ethel found us again through a couple who we were both close to, Maude and Andy Anderson. We all decided to have a reunion dinner at our house and we'd get to see everyone's children. We were very happily surprised when Ethel's long-time friends of her family, Gabrielle and Johnny Tait arrived with their new baby, Isabelle. It felt like we all had come home. Maude and Andy brought Joyce, newly born. By this time my Nathaniel was almost five and my Abby was almost four, and Bun and Ethel brought little Cora who was four and half and little new born, Billy. You lot were cute as buttons!

Maude put Joyce by us at the dining room table by Isabelle and Billy while you children were dining upstairs in the bedroom. I'd set up a table and we could hear so well through the ventilation screen in the ceiling. In older houses there were vents placed in the ceiling and if you looked up you could see right into the room above you. Unfortunately for us, you could see right down as well which provided many hours of entertainment for you children. Your father must have went up to read the riot act six times. Each time we would giggle at the table and we could hear him speaking very firmly to you children, telling you to play quietly, and also telling you not to come downstairs. Well, after the first course, your three little faces were pressed against the vent staring down at us and your father became worried the vent could give way. He shouted up at you children to go play and find something to do. Finally, he became so irritated that he rushed up there and you children panicked. We

were laughing so hard that we almost wet ourselves. We hushed and tried to listen.
"Nathaniel! Now, you get one smack!" Well, we heard it all the way down stairs.
"Abigail Gene get right on over here!"
Well, another smack!
"There! That'll teach you I mean business!"
Your father came down just in agony, clutching his hand.
"I tell you all that those kids are made of iron! Feels like I damn near broke my hand!"
Then we completely lost ourselves and you children were up there giggling about something which made things even worse or better depending on how you see things after a few glasses

of wine with long- time friends you haven't seen for ages.
Suddenly we could hear a dripping sound coming from somewhere. We then noticed that water was coming from the vent and dripping right onto the table.
Nathaniel shouted, "You better let us come down stairs!"
"No excuses young man! We're trying to enjoy our dinner. Now you find something to do with yourself!"
Your father's eyebrows squeezed together so tight, I thought they'd stay that way as he stared up into the vent. Then we watched as the drip quickly turned into a slow, steady stream of urine. If I hadn't been there myself I wouldn't have believed it! Sure enough as God is my witness, Nathan had peed right smack dab in the center of our dinner party. He had

said he needed to come down…Your father rushed up. Bun, Johnny, and Andy went with him. He grabbed Nathaniel and planted a good hard smack on his bottom and then he yelled in pain. Not Nathaniel, but your father!
"Oh sweet Jesus! If it hurts this much after I've had a few, just think what it'll feel like tomorrow! I think I've broken my hand! Boy! What have you got in there?"
Nathan still pulled over your father's knee, reached into the backside part of his pajama bottom and pulled out the hard book of Tom Sawyer and Huck Finn!
"Abby, darling, take the book out of your bottoms."
Me, Ethel, Gabrielle and Maude stared up through the floor. We each bit our bottom lip partly trying not to

laugh and then I remembered the only other book I had up there was the, Bible and sure enough.
"Figured I needed God on my side, Pa!"
Abby tried to explain her choice of defense.
"Is that a fact?"
"Yes sir. This side right here especially since I hurt it falling off a swing yesterday."
Ethel just about split her side laughing.
"Wait, just wait!" She whispered.
Bun went over to little Cora. He sat her on his knee and asked her if she had anything to say.
"Like what, Pa?"
"Like do you have a book in your bottoms?"
"Oh I wouldn't put a book there, Pa."
"Cora!"

"Oh alright!" She confessed hastily as she was pretty choked up by this time.
"They were plum out'a books!"
"Cora!"
She cried as she pointed to the table. There were only two place settings where there were obviously three at one time. Well that finished us.
"Cora, you know I almost broke my hand the last time you put a book in your bottoms!"
"Yes sir."
"Why on heaven's earth would you put a plate there this time?"
"Well, I figured you ain't learned noth'n since the last time!" She folded her arms, stomped her left foot and pouted.
Bun made Cora say sorry for teaching you children about the book thing to save bottoms from smacking. Nathan

said sorry for peeing through the vent and for putting the book in his bottom that almost broke his father's hand. Abby said sorry she didn't think of the book thing sooner so your father would stop smackings! It was one of the best nights of our lives. Good friends and family is what it's all about.

Strange as it might be, when we had time to talk properly, Ethel and I exchanged stories of how our first child died. Bun Jr. died in the night. Ethel told me she checked him almost every hour, being a new mother and all. He was two months old. When she found him he was cold and not moving. She said part of her died that day and she thanks God for Bun, Cora, Billy, and me. I told her about Hattie and we cried as only two friends who knew each other that well

*could. See, as loving as husbands are, and she and I had the best ones for us truly, there is nothing on heaven and earth like that girl friend who takes you for what you are, accepts you and understands you. Whatever I ever thought I'd try she supported me and loved me through distance, time and life. I did the same for her and when she died I missed her differently than your father. I could tell her things that I'd never dream of saying to your father. Things were just that way.
Gosh I'm going back a few years now, but when you all read these words you should all be so lucky as to have a Maude and Andy, Bun and Ethel, and a Johnny and Gabrielle. Then when you are old like me you won't feel let down because you've been loved well and you loved well. I still talk to Ethel like she's sitting right here beside me*

and since I'm the last of the bunch, I know I'll be greeted by good people I'm just dying to see. I had to put that last part in there 'cause Ethel would have laughed. So if you think of it that way, it's not so sad, or even so bad, really.
I did sort of think to myself once or twice to write a mystery like that Agatha Christie. I would have liked to become a published author. I would have liked to see my name on the cover of a book. That's the only thing I can say I thought of and never did. I don't regret not having done it but it's just a little something I would have liked to do. In my opinion there should always be something you might like to do some day. That way, it might get done if the timing is right. I suppose this entry became a little rambled. I really meant to talk about

my great friend Ethel, how I love your father, how wonderful my life has been, how I don't have regrets, and for you all to know how I feel so well loved and how I hope you all feel well loved by me.

It's every parent's dream for their children to have a happy life. My advice to you three children, full grown, children of your own, is to never stop seeing how beautiful things are right under your noses. Then you won't feel that pressure like you're going without something. We were dirt poor sometimes and we knew life was hard. We also knew never to take things for granted. I believe I started that well known expression, 'It could be worse.' After surviving war, hardship, death and poverty, I knew this to be true and saying it reminded me, and everyone else around me just how fortunate we were. Oh yes, I also am a very huge admirer of laughing as often as possible and if the situation doesn't present itself, smiling won't kill you neither!

Entry 45: This January 1946
 Mrs. Olivia Foxworthy

Chapter Six
When Clara Laughs

Chapter Six
When Clara Laughs

As you readers may well have guessed, my dear mother was quite a card.
When I asked her to write her memoirs after my father passed away, I never knew she ever did it. She was good at keeping secrets. After she passed the memoirs started turning up places. Apparently she scattered them around the house, stuffed them in books, in her knitting bag, in her closet, and this accounts for the lack of chronological order and lack of entries. They just keep turning up as time goes by. Each one we find is like gold to us. As her children, it's a thrill for us to read about our lives when we were young as seen through our mother's eyes. Because of this surprise, we ourselves have begun to keep journals to pass on to our children, which of course include copies of our mother's memoirs. Reading the pages, I couldn't help but wonder what she referred to when she said we were poor. Then I remembered we must have been, but we never felt without. It was just

her way to point out how fortunate we were, and how nice it felt to have each other.
My brothers and I know she always wanted to be a mystery writer and she swore she solved every mystery ever written. She always told us, "You never know what can happen! Big things can come from small potatoes like me! You just might be surprised to see my name on the cover of a book one day!" She always said it jokingly and it always made us smile. Now, wherever you are Momma, it's your turn to be surprised. We did this for you. Your name on the cover of your book, filled with your own words, just as you would have it. As happy as we think you'll be by this news, we couldn't live with ourselves imagining you up in heaven with even the slightest personal regret or goal that you may not have had time to get around to. That's how much we love you Momma and we miss you so very much every day.
Life is funny, isn't it? Nathan misses your chocolate chip cookies and sense of humor the most. Jonas misses your crazy phone calls trying to figure out speed dial on the phone, calling him up thinking you have the Chinese

food restaurant. Me, well I miss your apple crisp and a tear forms in my eyes every time my little Clara laughs right from the heart. She has your laugh Momma and that head of floppy curly hair. With everything you ever taught me, being a parent now, I hope that laugh carries her through thick and thin all her life.
Me and Nathan and Jonas would just like to have it in words that we are so grateful for having known you.
And yes Momma, we feel so well loved by you.

In loving memory, with all our hearts,

Nathaniel Marcus Foxworthy,
Abigail Foxworthy-Johnson,
Jonas James Foxworthy

And of course, our eldest sister,
little Harriet Foxworthy,
also known as Hattie.

Chapter Seven
Still Something Wanting

Chapter Seven
Still, Something Wanting...

Following my mother's funeral, people gathered at my mother's house. The mourning process showed its ugly head and seemed to ravage our family from youngster to senior. When everyone had gone, I wondered into my old bedroom. My mother always kept our bedrooms the same as when we were children so our children could see where we came from. My father said she was too damn sentimental. I can remember him, just a few years back, sitting on the end of my bed one time, just smiling, remembering the old days. I think it was just one of those things. It was one of those things Momma loved to tease him about and just loved about him.
I sat on the end of my bed just looking around. I found my old box of treasures. I decided to take it home for Clara to look through with me one rainy day in the future. I whispered, "Thank you, Momma..." as I left the room.

For the next few days, decisions would have to be made about the house, and other such matters. My brother's and I went through the house. We were supposed to be deciding what each of us wanted, but instead we just sat around in the kitchen talking, having coffee. When it was time to leave, my daughter Clara ran to me with my Momma's knitting bag. "Will you finish what Gramma started?" I looked into the bag and to my surprise, under the un- finished sweater for one of the kids, was Momma's Memoir about Jedidiah Brown. We stopped what we were doing, as I read aloud. We never knew, at least not the whole story. She never said. We were choked. I looked to my brother's and we smiled and laughed nervously. One decision was made. We were not selling this house, ever!

For the next few days, we met, and looked everywhere through old papers, books, dressing table drawers, and it was then we found, Sweetest of Angels. We stayed up through the night searching, in case there were any other siblings we needed to know about. It was like Easter egg hunting and we were giddy with excitement. It was almost like being children again.

The following day while cleaning out perishables, Nathan found Momma's Tuesday. Our reaction was of mixed emotion, coupled with disbelief, grief and shock. By the time we found Cookies from God we had lost ourselves in our past. We half expected Momma to come walking through that door at any moment and say, "I don't know why you are all so surprised! I said I would write'm if I had the time. What took you so long finding them?!"

That would have been just like her.

As it happens, the decisions were made with great ease and no bickering. We kept the house and used it as refuge, meeting house, sleepover headquarters for cousins and family. As said before we decided to have her Memoirs published. A difficult decision was what exactly to end the book with. I am the writer in the family and we decided I should write a little something explaining how and why we came to publish the Memoirs. That is how the chapter, When Clara Laughs, came to be. We found a publishing house and set the ball rolling, yet there was still something wanting. We couldn't put our fingers on it. We just felt like something was missing. And then as unpredictable as life is, my rainy day happened.

It was a particularly stormy September day when Clara and I sat down to look through my childhood box of treasures. We dusted it off and there were my old things. Clara giggled in that adorable bratty seven year old giggle like my mother's, "Didn't you have any real toys in the olden days mom?"

I giggled too. A huge marble, a few tarnished rings, an old necklace made of painted pasta noodles on a string, an old wad of chewing gum that I probably meant to return to later, a prayer card with Virgin Mary on it, tiny diary, and a crumpled piece of paper. Clara ran off to show her father what I played with in the olden days before there were real toys.

I slowly opened the old book.

"Momma is very cross at me for putting a spider in Nathan's soup today. He prit'near had a heart attack raising his spoon to his mouth seeing that big black spider look'n back at him. It was just great! I told her I did

it 'cause he called me Crabby Abby for two hours solid. So now we're punished from each other till we love each other better. Creep! Wonder what he's doing anyway!"
I laughed remembering. Kids can be so mean sometimes. I couldn't wait to let him read this. I flipped through old doodlings, a few jokes, some ripped out pages, and then I came to the next entry.
"Momma is very serious now. She got back a few days ago from her trip to her Uncle's farm. Today we went to visit Gramma at the graveyard. We had to dress sharp and we all brought flowers. Momma told us to stand back a bit while she put her flowers down, then she put down a little note into the earth. She walked off slowly and told us to put our flowers down and say good bye to Gramma. I went last and I snatched that note. I think I must be going to hell or something because it might be a sin to take mail away from dead people. I ran to my room and closed the door. I opened the paper and it didn't have much on it really. I'll keep it in my treasure box 'till I bring it back. Gosh! A girl goes through all the trouble of stealing mail from a dead

person and it ain't got nothing I can make out on it! Maybe I'll still go to heaven 'cause it's a very short note."

By the time I had written the next entry, I suppose I had discussed God with my mother…

"Momma says if a person asks God's forgiveness, he usually helps them out if the person really means to be forgiven. So I guess I'll sleep better tonight. God's not so bad after all I suppose. He really had me going for a while."

I hesitated as I unfolded the crumpled note carefully. My heart pounded as if it were the first time I read it. Memory flooded back to me as my eyes poured over words my mother had written to her own mother. Of course this time I knew more. This time, I couldn't ask for forgiveness, like I could when she was alive. This time would be very different. I read her note slowly.

"Dear Momma,

Thank you for forgiving me for not knowing how much you loved me when I was little. You went through great lengths to spare me pain you once knew as a child. We buried you

on a Tuesday, not on purpose, just so you know. Strange coincidence, maybe not. I could tell looking back now you forgave me after Aunt Ruth passed and now I know why. You forgave yourself too, didn't you? Maybe you didn't need to forgive me, but after that you could love me more easy like. You're brave Momma. I didn't know that about you. I hope you get my message and I'll talk to you in my prayers.
All my love and respect, your Olivia."

Tears streamed down my face. My heart sank. How I had disrespected my own mother by taking this note! How sorry I was! If only I could turn back the hands of time, I'd return that note! What had I done? I ran into the washroom and slammed the door crying, with guilt and shame. Several moments passed when Clara came to the door worried, diary in hand. "Momma, are you crying 'cause Gramma Olivia wrote in your diary when it's s'posed to be private?"
I opened the door slowly. She handed me the diary. "Don't be sad, Momma. Me and Daddy

are making you a Shirley Temple like in the restaurant!"

With red, swollen and puffy eyes, I read those words that changed me forever.

"Dear Crabby Abby. (Just joking with you)
Dear Abigail,

Just what are you doing worrying like this? How could you forget for one minute how much I love you? I know you took the note. Mothers have eyes in the backs of our heads. I knew since the day at the graveyard you took that note. But you kept it in your treasure box and one day, when you're older, it'll mean something to you. You are curious, not evil, my dear. You're gonna be my little girl long after I die and I'll always love you, even then. 'Course it's wrong to take things that are not yours, but I forgive you and if I want to talk to my mother, I pray and talk to her direct-like. So never worry, she got my message long before I ever wrote it. I'm glad your snoopy brother secretly found your diary and I hope you read this soon.

Do not waste God given time on this precious earth with hard feelings, my love. Show yourself the respect you deserve and never

deny yourself of your loved ones who value
you so dearly. See, when you live this way, and
I hope I taught you well, the love just keeps
making its rounds, never beginning, never
ending.
Yes, your brother is punished but only half
being on account of him only being half a
snoopy brother and half a worried brother.
He's punished for the snoopy half. You see
how it works?
You were so worried with hard feelings, you
deprived yourself of your brother who
incidentally missed you in his life. He set out
to fix the situation and since you wouldn't talk
to him, he read your diary.
No more hard feelings.

I'm make'n your favorite apple crisp.
Love, Momma."
I just sat on washroom floor weeping. I never
found her note to me and to find it now, all
these years later…
Clara came down the hall giggling, carrying a
tray, spilling drops all the way. She put the
tray down on the floor. She bent over with
her hands on her knees and leaned into me

and whispered, "I had hoped to have a picnic outside, but with the weather and you bawling here, guess the washroom is as good a place as any."

She wiped away a tear from my cheek. She stretched out a bath towel on the floor, placed out our drinks and there we sat cross-legged on the washroom floor. She looked at my husband, and then at me, and started laughing the laugh as she wiped her mouth with her hands after taking a big drink.

"Well?! Are we any having fun yet? You want to make some more of those funny toys of yours?" Of course, we all laughed..

Who could want for anything more?
Thank you, Momma.

Author's Notes:

Author's Notes:

All the while writing this little book I kept family and friends so close to my heart. Big things can come from small potatoes, and I grew up believing that anything is actually possible. Just because something hasn't been done yet, doesn't mean it won't get done at all. As Olivia would say, "You don't know what you can't do, so why on God's green earth would yah let someone else tell you what you are not capable of? Give it a go and see what happens. Knowledge can be acquired, skill can be attained, and will is God's gift to us all. That's how things get done."

For all who read this little book into someone's opinion of their own life, I hope for laughter, tears, joy, and a

distinct fondness for the appreciation of life, witnessing what the human spirit can endure.
It is with great pride that I re-introduce The Memoirs of Mrs. Olivia Foxworthy to the world in its 2nd Edition.

Second Author's Note:

Dear Reader,
As much as I wish it were true, The Memoirs of Mrs. Olivia Foxworthy is actually a complete work of fiction. Still, wouldn't it be just a little bit special if Olivia was real, her words, unvarnished and so wonderful?

Maybe there is a bit of Olivia within each of our hearts and maybe that will make her real enough.

Her memory, character, pains and joys feel real to me as anyone could possibly be and I am very happy to share.

- Alex McLellan

About The Author

Author, Illustrator, Photographer, and Entrepreneur, Alex McLellan lives in Shelburne, Ontario, Canada, with her loving husband and beautiful Co-Author, Miles, the Cat.

*"I write because I have to write. Writing is a compulsion for me, an addiction, an inexplicable power, steeling the imagination, creating a doorway into another world where anything can happen.
Who if given a choice would not choose to live in such a world?"*
-Alex McLellan

*Other Works By This Author
Available on Amazon Include:*

*Children's Books Also Include
Coloring Pages*

New Book
By Local Author
Alex McLellan
Now Available On
Amazon
Cobwebs & Caviar!

Books Can Be Borrowed From The
Shelburne Public Library

*Books By Alex McLellan (Kimmi)
are also currently available at
BookLore in Orangeville, ON.*

Contact:
Twitter: @AKMcLellanBooks
Facebook: Alex McLellan Books
Website: alexmclellanbooks.com
Email:
alexmclellanbooks@gmail.com

Acknowledgements:
Special Thanks To Nathan Sher for
Technical Support & Editing
& Cover Layout

Front And Back Cover Photography
By Alex McLellan

Location of Book Cover:
Mono, Ontario, Canada

Layout for book cover with help from
Canva found at httsp://www.canva.co
Copyright 2020©
Alex McLellan

Shelburne Public Library
201 Owen Sound Street
Shelburne, ON L9V 3L2

Made in the USA
Monee, IL
16 February 2021

59637032R00073